HERCULES

The Story of

An Old-Fashioned Fire Engine

Written and   *Illustrated by*

Hardie Gramatky

Author of "**LITTLE TOOT**"

G.P. Putnam's Sons   *New York*

Copyright © 1940, renewed © 1968, by Hardie Gramatky.
All rights reserved. Published simultaneously in Canada
by Academic Press Canada Limited, Toronto.
Printed in the United States of America.
Fifteenth Impression
Library of Congress Cataloging in Publication Data
Gramatky, Hardie.
Hercules; the story of an old-fashioned fire engine.
I. Title.   PZ7.G7654He   40-34108
ISBN 0-399-60240-2 GB
ISBN 0-399-20728-7 pbk.

First Peppercorn paperback edition
published in 1980.

To

ANNE AND REX MURPHY

This is the story of Hercules, a famous fire engine. When *your* grandfather was young, he and his friends thought that Hercules was one of the finest fire engines ever built. Then nobody had ever heard of a fire truck.

It wasn't so long ago, either.

Today Hercules is in a museum. Had it not been for a wonderful act of courage— and a little luck—he never would have won such a fine place.

This is how it happened. The day Hercules came from the factory the whole town turned out; and the Mayor made a long speech and proudly referred to Hercules as "the most modern, the most up-to-date fire engine in the world."

It was a proud day for Hercules. His brass gleamed, his safety valve danced, and the quivering needle on the steam gauge showed how strong he was.

Hercules was drawn by three horses —one black, one white, and one dapple-gray. And the people of the town presented him with a mascot, a spotted coach dog to run with him to the fires.

Hercules had a crew of three — Hokey, Pokey, and Smokey. Hokey was the fireman. He kept steam up in the big boiler.

Pokey was engineer. He watched the gauges and connected the hose to hydrants.

And Smokey sat on the front seat and drove the horses.

They made a great team. People used to
hang around the firehouse for hours on
end, on the chance an alarm might ring.

It was exciting to see the horses leap
toward their harness when the gong struck.

It was even more exciting to see them
in full flight through the town.

And it was most exciting of all to see how quickly they put out a fire. One blast of water from Hercules' hose and it was all over.

Anyhow, that's how it was in the beginning. The trouble was that time was passing, and new things were being invented.

There was a strange, noisy vehicle—the automobile. People called it a "horseless carriage."

It was almost too much for
the horses....

Hokey didn't like the looks of this at all. "First thing you know," he said, "they'll be puttin' motors in fire engines. And when they do that Hercules and all of us are done for."

But Smokey and Pokey said he was plumb crazy. Smokey jeered, "We'll stick by Hercules and our horses. At least with them we'll always get to the fire."

This was true. But Smokey, in his pride and affection, had over-looked the simple fact that with a fire engine what counts above everything else is getting to a fire *first.*

For there came a day...

when Hercules, though he rolled as fast
as ever, arrived too late.

The fire was out.

It had been put out by a new kind of
fire engine—an engine that wasn't pulled
by horses at all.

This new-fangled machine chugged under its own power. Already one of these monsters was coming back from the fire and at the top of the hill Hercules met him face to face.

The upstart blasted his exhaust in Hercules' face and nearly choked him to death.

Life was unbearable after that. The Aldermen and the Mayor solemnly decided that Hercules was "obsolete." He was too old — too slow. So they retired him.

From then on nothing seemed to happen. The alarm never sounded.

The horses were sold—the black one to a riding academy, the dapple-gray to a junk dealer, and the white one to the police force.

And Hercules grew old like a soldier pining for the smell of gunpowder.

But Hokey, Pokey, and Smokey, because they loved the firehouse, stayed on.

"Wait and see," said Smokey, "someday there's goin' to be a fire—the worst fire this city ever saw. An' we'll be there —with Hercules. There's things that Hercules and horses can do that those trucks can't do."

That day came sooner than even Smokey had
dared to hope. Their own alarm suddenly sounded. The cobwebs flew in all directions.

"It's a general alarm," yelled Smokey. "The
City Hall. We've got to do something." How-
ever, there were no horses to pull Hercules.

But he knew what to do—he began to ring his
big brass bell.

When the old black horse heard that familiar clang, he shot like a bolt from under his gentleman rider, and tore to the firehouse.

The dapple-gray aban-
doned his junk wagon.

And the white horse just
brought his new master right
in with him.

"Here they come," yelled
Pokey.

This was like old times. . . .

It was a good thing they started; and before long they found out why. One after another, all the fire trucks, which weren't so dependable in those days, had come to grief. First they passed Hose No. 4. No. 4's crew were cranking their heads off, but the engine wouldn't start.

"We can use that hose," yelled Hokey.

They stopped only long enough to pick

it up.

Then they overtook Hook
and Ladder No. 1. No. 1 had
blown a tire, then the spare,
and the crew were sweating
to pump it up.

"Never mind that," Smokey bellowed.

"Get aboard with the ladder."

Emergency Truck No. 3 was hopelessly stuck in a muddy ditch.

"Get aboard," Pokey yelled to the dumfounded crew, "and bring your life net."

On the steep hill near the City Hall they heaved past Chemical No. 2. It just didn't have the power to get up the slope.

Hercules could do things

that no fire truck could *ever*

hope to do. . . .

The bridge was out, but . . .

Hercules never stopped. . . .

This was the worst fire he had ever seen. The heat was so scorching that Pokey had to unharness the horses and lead them away.

If they were to save the City Hall, Hercules had to pump water as he had never pumped before. While Hokey fed coal under the boiler, Pokey threw himself on the safety valve, and Hercules pumped until he was *blue* in the face.

Everyone was saved, including the Mayor and the Aldermen, with no hurt except to their dignity.

And that was how Hercules

got into the Museum.